D1485579

Happy Ever After

For Felix

S.W.

ORCHARD BOOKS
338 Euston Road, London NW1 3BH
Orchard Books Australia
Hachette Children's Books
Level 17/207 Kent Street, Sydney, NSW 2000
ISBN 1 84362 527 X (hardback)
ISBN 1 84362 535 0 (paperback)
First published in Great Britain in 2006
First paperback publication in 2006
Text © Tony Bradman 2006
Illustrations © Sarah Warburton 2006
The rights of Tony Bradman to be identified as the author
and of Sarah Warburton to be identified as the illustrator of this
work have been asserted by them in accordance with the
Copyright, Designs and Patents Act, 1988.
A CIP catalogue record for this book is available
from the British Library.
1 3 5 7 9 10 8 6 4 2 (hardback)
1 3 5 7 9 10 8 6 4 2 (paperback)
Printed in Great Britain

Tony Bradman

Happy Ever After

THE FROG PRINCE
HOPS TO IT

Illustrated by Sarah Warburton

ORCHARD BOOKS

Prince Freddy eased open the back door of the royal mansion and slipped inside. He tiptoed down a corridor...

...paused at a door to make sure there was no one around...

...and dashed across the hall.

"Phew, made it!" he thought as he began to climb the stairs. But suddenly a shadow fell across him.

He looked up, and gulped. His lovely wife, Princess Daisy, was scowling down at him from the landing.

"Huh, so you've finally bothered to come home," she muttered.

"Listen, darling," said Prince Freddy. "I can explain, honest."

"Don't bother," Daisy said. "I know where you've been. You're covered in mud and you smell gross. When are you going to realise that you're not a frog any more, Freddy?"

Freddy sighed. He had been a frog for a time - or rather, a prince who had been transformed into a frog by the Wicked Witch.

He had gone to live at the big pond, but then he'd met Daisy at a local well.

Eventually she had freed him from the curse with a kiss, and they were married. And to begin with they had been blissfully happy.

But now it seemed they didn't really
have much in common.

Daisy had become interested in doing
charity work, and she was terribly busy.

She was always getting involved in
campaigns for good causes such as the
Fading Fairy Fund, the Hansel and
Gretel Kids-In-Trouble Helpline, even
the Keep-the-Forest-Clean-and-Green
Appeal.

And Freddy wasn't exactly sure *what*
he liked doing now he was a person
again. He had really enjoyed being
a frog, and he missed it. He missed the
pond and his froggy friends, too.

"Er...I know I'm not a frog any more, Daisy," Freddy said. "I just like spending time down at the big pond, that's all. What's wrong with that?"

"Nothing, I suppose," Daisy said. "At least not if you think hanging round a smelly old pond is a good idea, that is."

"But I don't. I think it's a bit wet. I wish you could find something more serious to do. Now if you'll excuse me, I have some important letters to write."

And with that, Daisy turned on her heel and stomped off to her office.

Freddy trudged upstairs to their bedroom. Of course he knew that Daisy didn't like him going to the big pond - which is why he'd taken to sneaking there in secret recently.

16

But that obviously hadn't worked.
And he hated deceiving her. It just
didn't feel right.

Freddy decided to have a bath. As he wallowed in the water, he wondered what to do. He loved Daisy, and he thought she still loved him. But he loved the big pond too. If only Daisy felt the same way about it.

He was sure she would - if only she
understood how amazing it was...

So why didn't he show her? "Yes, that's it!" he said, and leaped out of the bath.

He threw on some clothes and sat at his own little desk.

Then he glanced at the calendar on the wall. Daisy's birthday was coming up in a few weeks. "Even better!" he thought, and started making plans...

The morning of Daisy's birthday arrived at last. When she woke up, Freddy gave her a huge birthday card.

Then he led her down to the royal dining room, where there was an enormous heap of presents.

"Are these all for me?" said Daisy.
"You shouldn't have, Freddy."

She gave him a lovely smile, the kind
he hadn't seen for too long.

"Well, aren't you going to open
them?" said Freddy, smiling back.

Daisy picked up a present and quickly ripped off the wrapping paper.

"Oh, it's a book," she murmured, her smile fading. "About...ponds."

"Yes, and it's got some really marvellous pictures in it," Freddy said.

There were more books too, including
Fairy Tale Ponds, *Life On A Lily Pad*
and *Time for Slime*.

There were DVDs about ponds, a pond poster, a special Pond-Watcher's Kit...even a pair of frog-shaped slippers, just for fun.

Daisy's smile vanished entirely, and her bottom lip quivered.

"Well," said Freddy, realising that he might have made a mistake, "I was planning to take you for a lovely picnic at, er...the big pond."

"I don't believe it!" Daisy wailed.
"This is the worst birthday I've ever had.
I'm beginning to wonder why I married
you in the first place. You're going
to have to make your mind up,
Freddy - it's that pond...or me!"

Then she burst into tears and ran out.
Freddy followed and tried to talk to her,
but she had locked herself in her office
and refused to see him...

That afternoon, Freddy trudged off
to say a final goodbye to the big pond.
He had made his choice, but he still
felt sad.

He stood by the cool green water, listened to the insects buzzing and the soft, plopping sounds as his froggy friends dived in...then he heard another sound...a banging.

A man was putting up a sign nearby.

Suddenly Freddy felt rather uneasy.

"Er, hi," he said. "Would you mind telling me what that means?"

"Sure," said the man. "We're putting an eight-lane highway through here soon - the forest bypass. We start draining the pond tomorrow."

Freddy was horrified. "But...but...you can't do that!" he said. "What's going to happen to all the creatures who live in it?"

"Not my problem, mate," said the man, and walked off. "Cheerio!"

Freddy was angry now. Even if he
never went to the big pond again,
he just had to save it and his friends!
But how? Then it came to him, and
he smiled.

He couldn't do it on his own.
He needed to launch a massive
campaign - and he knew just the
person to help him get it organised.

Freddy ran home as fast as he could,
and soon he was standing outside
Daisy's office door again. He raised his
hand to knock, but then he paused...

What if Daisy thought it was good riddance to the big pond? What if she didn't want to be involved?

But somehow Freddy had a feeling that she would - so long as he could persuade her to talk to him. In the end she opened her door as soon as she heard the words "good cause".

"An eight-lane highway!" she said, just as appalled as Freddy. "Of course I'll help. It might only be a smelly old pond, but destroying it would be a total disaster for the forest environment!

"Now let me see - we'll have to make some posters, put together a petition, and organise a demonstration..." And thus the 'Save The Big Pond' campaign was born.

Daisy threw herself into it with all her usual energy. She read the books Freddy had given her, and was amazed at how many different varieties of frog there were.

"That would be useful for the posters," she thought.

She watched the DVDs, too, and they gave her the idea for *Wet Rock - The Concert To Save The Big Pond.*

And she even went to the big pond
with Freddy, where her special
pond-watcher's kit came in very useful.
(Although she never did wear the
frog-shaped slippers, not once.)

The campaign was a total success, and the big pond was saved forever. Freddy was delighted, but he also realised that he had absolutely loved working on it. So he asked Daisy if he could help with her other good causes, too.

He took everything very seriously, and worked just as hard as Daisy, and they became a terrific, unbeatable team. (Although they made sure they always had plenty of fun as well.)

So Daisy and Freddy and their froggy friends really did live...HAPPILY EVER AFTER!

Written by Tony Bradman
Illustrated by Sarah Warburton

These books are available from all good bookshops, or can be ordered direct
from the publisher: Orchard Books, PO BOX 29, Douglas IM99 1BQ.
Credit card orders please telephone 01624 836000 or fax 01624 837033 or
visit our Internet site: www.wattspub.co.uk or
e-mail: bookshop@enterprise.net for details.

To order please quote title, author and ISBN and your full name and
address. Cheques and postal orders should be made payable to 'Bookpost
plc.' Postage and packing is FREE within the UK
(overseas customers should add £1.00 per book).

Prices and availability are subject to change.